A "FIT"ting Fairy Tale

Kathryn A. Brave, M.A.
Paul J. Lavin, Ph.D.

PublishAmerica
Baltimore

D1714055

First printing

All characters appearing in this work are fictitious. Any resemblance to real persons, living or dead, is purely coincidental.

ISBN: 1-4241-2992-3
PUBLISHED BY PUBLISHAMERICA, LLLP
www.publishamerica.com
Baltimore

Printed in the United States of America

To Naim:

For saying the book was funny "even without pictures."

A
"FIT"ting
Fairy Tale

Chapter One:
A Wicked Plan

Years ago, in the land of Lipids, there lived a cowardly man whose only wish was to please his selfish wife. He worked very hard hoping to bestow upon her all the riches of the world. Yet still she was unhappy.

One night, as she was tossing and turning in her sleep, he woke her and asked, "What is troubling you, my dear?"

Angry as always, she snapped at her loving husband, "It's those ridiculous children! They want me to feed them and take care of them! And oh, how awful," she cried. "They want me to wash their dirty laundry!"

The man, who loved his children very much, looked at the woman and sighed, "But they are our children. Shouldn't we try to make them happy?"

The woman rolled her eyes and cried out, "If we continue to spend money on them, we will never have enough for ourselves. And I refuse to live in poverty when I am old and wrinkled!"

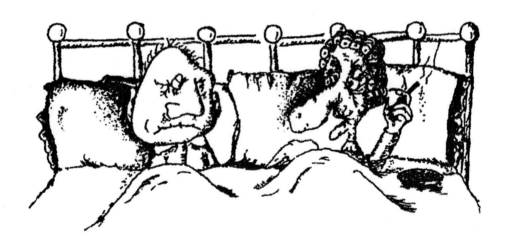

Now, what the stepmother did not realize was that she was no longer the beautiful woman she once was. For years she had eaten at every fast food restaurant under the sun. She had gorged on greasy French fries covered in mayonnaise, and smoked just enough to make her seem as if she was a smoldering chimney. And after all that, she had become an old, wrinkled witch of a woman.

"I have a wonderful idea," she whispered. "Tomorrow we will take the children for a hike in the forest. When night falls, we will leave them for the wolves and the bears. This way we will be free of them forever."

The man sighed. "I can not do that," he said. You see, he was starting to become courageous. But then, as always, he backed down.

"I made a promise to love you and keep you happy for life," he sighed. "And so if you believe that this is the right thing, then we will take Hansel and Gretel into the woods at sunup."

Now, what the man and his wife did not know was that Hansel and Gretel, two very hungry children, had awakened for a midnight snack. As they shoved themselves full of chocolate donuts and French fries, they overheard what their stepmother was saying.

"No more fried chicken," blubbered Gretel. "No more taco surprise! No more Burger Barn! And...and...and....." She could hardly catch her breath. "Hansel," she howled as she held up a powdered sugar doughnut, "no more frosted doughnuts!"

Hansel knew that he must do something. But after all

those sweets, he felt tired and confused. He tried to think, but his mind was fuzzy. And so, as his little sister let out cries of sadness, he fell fast asleep in the middle of the kitchen floor.

Chapter Two:
Leaving Lipids

The stepmother was moving about the house hastily, screaming at the top of her lungs. "Get up!" she hollered as she tossed Gretel's shoes across the kitchen floor. "Get up and get dressed! We are going for a hike." Her stepmother stood before her dressed in her highest heels and a pink mini-dress. "Let's move!" she cried out. Furiously, she dragged Hansel to his bedroom and pulled a sweatshirt over his head.

"Gretel," she commanded, "go into the kitchen and get me some water! If I am going to stay young and beautiful, I need water!"

Everyone knew that Gretel was hardly the brighter of the two children. Yet still she remembered her parents' conversation from the night before. And so she decided to cook up a master plan. She began looking for leftover burgers, fried chicken and hash browns. If I am going to die, thought Gretel, I will never let myself die of starvation.

She opened the refrigerator and grabbed a leftover carton of fried chicken nuggets. She took out each nugget, sniffed it and shoved it deep into her pocket. Then she scampered to the kitchen sink, where she quickly filled up a glass of cold water.

Frantically, Gretel raced into the living room and placed the cup in the hands of her evil stepmother. The stepmother, as always, was dissatisfied.

"How long does it take to get a glass of water?" she hollered. "What in the world is wrong with you?"

Angrily she slammed the water down on the coffee table, spilling its contents all over the floor. Then she grabbed Gretel by the arm and dragged her out to the car, where Hansel and her father were waiting patiently.

Chapter Three:
The Trail of Nuggets

The husband drove, yet for some reason it seemed rather clear that the wife should have been the driver. "Turn right!" she commanded. "Turn left! Stop the car! Now! Stop the car!"

The car came to a screeching halt. Hansel and Gretel peered out the window. All they could see were the eerie shadows of the evergreen trees. Immediately a feeling of hopelessness came over them.

"This is it!" shouted the stepmother. "It is here that we will begin our journey." It was then that she pulled the children from the car and pushed them toward the deepest, darkest part of the forest.

As the family trudged along, Gretel did everything in her power to keep herself from thinking about the chicken nuggets that were nestled deep in her pocket. She thought about the new frosty taco ice cream dessert she had seen on T.V. She imagined herself living in a house made of candy with clear sugar windows and a gingerbread roof. But none of these delicious thoughts could keep her mind off of the fried chicken nuggets that fit so snugly in her pocket.

Gretel peered up at her stepmother. She thought that maybe she could sneak one nugget into her mouth when she wasn't looking. Carefully, she reached into her pocket. She took out one nugget. She placed it in her mouth, then another and another.

But what Gretel didn't realize was that each time she pulled a nugget from her pocket, a few of the other nuggets fell out onto the ground. This left a trail of chicken nuggets behind her as she walked deeper and deeper into the forest.

As they continued their hike into the darkest part of the forest, the birds circled above them in wonder. One bird in particular followed behind Gretel as she anxiously followed the narrow path.

This was not a magical bird, nor did it hope to become a friend to Gretel. But with each and every step, when greedy little Gretel dropped a fried chicken nugget from her pocket, the bird would snatch it up. Then he would gulp it down in one bite.

As Gretel walked along dropping nuggets, the bird followed closely behind her. It ate nugget after nugget after nugget. And with each bite, the bird grew heavier and heavier and weaker and weaker, until it finally became the broadest bird in the sky.

You see, what the bird didn't know was that each fried nugget was filled with a bad kind of fat called saturated fat. The more saturated fat the bird ate, the more clogged its itty-bitty birdie veins became. This made the bird much more unhealthy than it had ever been before.

Fortunately, the stepmother had not yet noticed the bird, nor had she caught Gretel eating the nuggets. She knew that Hansel was the smarter of the two children. Therefore, she focused all of her attention on the boy.

When night fell, the woman grew tired. She stopped and commanded her husband to go deep into the woods to fetch firewood.

She then turned to the children. "My darlings," she said, "why don't you lay down your precious little heads and take a rest? Then when you wake, we will continue our journey." Too exhausted to continue, Hansel and Gretel huddled together and fell fast asleep on the forest floor.

Chapter Four:
Tit for Tat

After she was sure that her children were dreaming, the woman paced about, cursing her husband for his stupidity. "How long does it take to gather firewood?" she grumbled.

Meanwhile, above her on a small branch, the bird that had been following Gretel sat quietly. It could no longer fly, for it had grown lethargic from eating all of those chicken nuggets. So instead it perched itself on a tiny tree branch and waited for morning.

The bird sat patiently, watching and waiting. It could feel the tree limbs cracking beneath it. The evil stepmother could also hear the breaking of the branches.

"This is ridiculous," she muttered. "Why is that tree making such outlandish noises?"

That's when she looked up toward the top of the tree and WAM! the branch snapped!

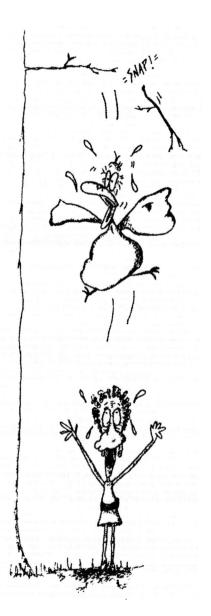

All she could see was an enormous bird falling straight out of the sky. Immediately she began to howl, but the bird fell...

Faster...

And faster...

And faster...

And faster...

Until...

SPLAT! It landed right on top of her!

It was so heavy that it pushed her underground with one swift landing, leaving her stuck inside the earth for the rest of eternity. There she resided with an angry little man named Rumplestiltskin, who never, ever let her have her way. And fortunately for Hansel and Gretel, she was never to be heard from again.

Chapter Five:
The House of Cholesterol

Although their stepmother was gone, Hansel and Gretel continued to dream. They dreamt of candy houses, cinnamon-covered pretzels, and happy families. They slept quietly through the night, only to find themselves alone in the woods the very next morning.

After realizing that they were all alone, Gretel began to cry. "Hansel," she blubbered, "we will never make it home alive!"

Just then, a giant bird waddled over and stood beside her.

"Gretel," said Hansel, "look! The bird! It's trying to tell us something!"

"Maybe it knows the way home!" cried Gretel.

Believing this to be true, the two children followed the bird as it waddled deeper into the forest, until they came upon a small house hidden among the trees.

As they approached the house, they noticed that it was built of chocolate chip cookies and covered with donuts. The windows were made of clear sugar.

"Hansel!" squealed Gretel. "It's the house in my dreams!"

With this she reached out and grabbed a chocolate-covered donut. She sniffed it. Then she gulped it down in one bite! After that, she began nibbling on a frosted wheat doughnut.

That is when the two children heard a voice coming from inside the house:

"Chomp, chomp, eat, eat,
Who is nibbling on my wheat?"

Now, most children would have answered with a clever response, but not Hansel and Gretel. They were too busy stuffing themselves with sweets. Hansel began tearing the chocolate chips from the cookies and shoving them into his mouth.

Suddenly, the door of the house flew open, and out hobbled a woman with more wrinkles than a raisin. Gretel was so scared that she actually dropped a jelly stick from her pudgy little hands.

Chapter Six:

Never Judge a Book by Its Cover

The old woman turned to the two children. "Please come in," she said. "You will be safe in my home." Thrilled with the thought of living in a candy house, Hansel and Gretel entered her home.

Inside they found a breakfast of pancakes, egg and sausage biscuits and hash browns. They had only dreamed of such a feast.

They devoured the meal, excusing themselves only to

get a nibble of the chocolate-covered chairs. "We must be in heaven," whispered Gretel.

Yet what they didn't know was that the witch's house was far from heaven. The witch was evil...very evil. She would often bring children into her home, fatten them up with sausage and cheese biscuits, and then eat them.

The more Hansel and Gretel ate, the more excited she became, singing to herself:

"Sausage, pancakes, donuts with yeast,
Soon I will have me a gigantic feast!"

That afternoon, as Gretel sipped on a chocolate shake, the witch opened the door of her tiny house and grabbed her by the arm. Then she locked her in a narrow cage in the gloomiest corner of the cellar. After that, she dropped the key deep into her pocket.

"My darling child," she snickered, "you can scream all you like, but no one will ever hear you!" And with that, she slammed the basement door behind her, leaving Gretel alone in the dark.

She later found Hansel outside, drinking from the caramel cream lake. Normally she would have sent the second child out to complete her chores, but not Hansel. Hansel had grown as plump as a Thanksgiving turkey, and the witch knew that the holidays were just around the corner. Her mouth began to water.

She grabbed him by the pudgy little arm and dragged him to a tiny shack in the forest. There, she shoved him into a cage made of steel bars.

"You may scream as much as you like," she snickered, "but only the rabbits and the turtles will hear you!" Then she slammed the door shut with a BANG! And off she hobbled into the wilderness.

Chapter Seven:
A Little Help from a Hare

Hansel began to sob uncontrollably, when suddenly he heard a voice from outside of the cage.

"Do not give up, my friend! You must try to save yourself."

Hansel peered out between the thick steel bars. There below him, directly at his feet, sat a tiny tortoise.

Hansel continued to cry. Tiny tears began rolling down his cheeks, spattering on the filthy cage floor.

That's when he heard voices from every corner of the shack.

"You must keep trying!"

"You mustn't give up!"

"You mustn't let her win!"

"She is evil!"

"We can stop her!"

A long-legged hare hopped over from a pile of cinders. "Stop your blubbering," he said. "We can help you!"

Hansel continued to cry. "How can you help me?" he asked. "You are just...just...just...animals."

The tortoise spoke first. "First," he said, "you need to get yourself in shape. Eat healthy—"

"And secondly," interrupted the hare, "you need to get some exercise! Get that heart pumping! Get that blood flowing! And for Pete's sake," he said, "maybe if you had some muscles, you could break free from that cage! Even we animals know that!"

All of the other animals nodded their heads.

"That's right! He needs muscles!" they squeaked.

"He needs to eat healthy!"

"He needs to get regular exercise!"

And so Hansel agreed to change his lifestyle, hoping to save Gretel before it was too late.

Chapter Eight:
The Great Escape

The plan went into effect almost immediately. Each night, the tortoise would bring Hansel vegetables from the witch's garden. The hare would steal meat or fish from the witch's dinner plate when she was not looking. You see, the hare had very long legs and was incredibly quick; therefore, he was able to steal almost anything. And sometimes at night, after Hansel had eaten right, the hare would steal a cookie for him. Luckily, the tortoise and the hare both knew that sweets could be eaten every once in a while.

Each morning before sunrise the tortoise and the hare would lead Hansel and the other animals in an exercise session. They would dance. The hare was particularly fond of hip-hop. They would do push-ups to build Hansel's muscles. And sometimes they would have races running in place. The tortoise was always the winner.

Hansel looked forward to his morning workouts. In fact, he was having fun and he was beginning to feel much stronger. Then, each evening after dinner, he would try to bend back the bars of the cage. Unfortunately, the bars were always much too strong for Hansel to move.

With each and every day, Hansel became more and more concerned. *Is it hopeless?* he wondered. *Will I ever escape?* The tension was increasing by the minute, when finally he realized that he may never see his sister again.

But then, after a few weeks of eating right and exercising, the rabbits approached Hansel. "Hansel," they cried, "we heard the witch talking and...and...and...." They could hardly control themselves. "She is planning to eat Gretel! Tonight!"

Hansel thought about what the hare would have told him to do: "Use your strength, boy! Use your strength!"

He flexed his newly formed muscles and grabbed hold of the bars.

"You can do it!" cried the rabbits.

"Persevere!" shouted the tortoise.

Hansel began to push out on the bars, and to his surprise they slowly began to bend.

"Keep pushing!" cried the hare.

"You got it!" shouted the tortoise.

He pushed and he pulled; and he pushed and he pulled until finally he had created a hole in the cage. Once the hole was large enough, he squeezed out between two bars. Then hastily he turned to the other animals.

"You," he said to the hare, "you can steal the key from the witch! And you," he pointed to the turtle, "you will make a wonderful look-out!"

And with no time to waste, the three friends ran off to the witch's house to save Gretel.

The witch had fallen fast asleep that evening. Hansel could see the key sticking out of her front pocket. This made it very easy for the hare to steal it.

Hansel took the key and slowly tiptoed down the stairs. He found Gretel sitting alone in the cage.

"Hansel!" she cried. "Hurry! Open the door before she wakes up!"

Hansel unlocked the door and out climbed Gretel. The two children crept up the stairs quietly and tiptoed out the front door. Then they took one giant leap and began the race of their lives.

Sensing the commotion, the evil witch awoke from her deep sleep. Hastily she began hobbling after the children, screaming:

"You nasty little children, you've ruined my feast,
Of plump Hansel pudding and Gretel with yeast!"

She was so incredibly loud that she woke one of the three bears who was hibernating in a nearby cave. Annoyed by her earsplitting tone, the giant bear waddled over and devoured her in one massive mouthful.

Meanwhile, Hansel and Gretel had run far from the house. Along the way, Gretel stopped and turned to Hansel. "Hansel," she said, "don't you want to take a cookie with you?"

Hansel thought about the tortoise and the hare and began to giggle. "No thanks," he said. "I think I'd rather have a carrot."

And with that, the two children continued running deep into the forest until they spotted three rather plump pigs sitting by a bubbly black stream.

Chapter Nine:
Who's Afraid of the Big Bad Wolf?

The first pig pulled a cigar from his mouth and shoved in a handful of potato chips. "So who's that guy think he is anyway?" he asked.

The second pig shook his head. "He thinks he's all big and bad and stuff."

"Well," said the third pig, "I ain't afraid of the big bad wolf!" He turned over and began sunbathing his backside.

"Wait a second!" said the first pig. "Who says I'm afraid of the big bad wolf?"

"Yeah," agreed the second pig, "we ain't afraid of the big bad wolf!"

"That's right," the first and second pig sang together. "We ain't afraid of nothin'! And if that big bad wolf came back up in here, why we'd...we'd...we'd get him! That's right! We'd get him!"

The third pig began to giggle. You see, he knew that his brothers were afraid of everything, especially the big bad wolf.

"All right then," he said, "if you two ain't afraid, then maybe *you* should go to the big bad wolf's house and...and—"

"And what?" asked the first pig.

"And what?" asked the second pig.

The third pig covered his mouth with his hoof. "Shhh," he whispered as he motioned toward the trees.

A very unfamiliar sound was coming from the north. It sounded like children.

Chapter Ten:
Humans!

The three plump pigs stood up slowly and stared into the brush. As they pushed at one another, trying to get a better look, the first pig spotted a most disturbing sight.

"Look," he whispered. "Humans."

You see, the three plump pigs were deathly afraid of humans. They wanted to eat chips, smoke cigars, lounge by the brook and stuff themselves with cheese curls. The last thing they wanted was to become the sausage patty on someone's greasy egg sandwich.

"Hide! Quick!" cried the first pig.

In a panic, he and the second pig began pushing one another out of the way, calling each other names.

"Humans!" they cried as they pulled one another back and forth. "Humans!"

"Move it!"

"Outta my way!"

"You bacon!"

"You sausage!"

"You...you...you...you fried ham!"

Sensing the commotion, Hansel and Gretel peered through the trees and began moving closer and closer to the three plump pigs.

"Close your eyes!" cried the second pig. "Then they won't see us!"

"Pretend you're a tree!" cried the first pig. "Then they won't recognize us!"

The third pig shook his head in disbelief. Not only were his brothers cowards, but did they also have to be idiots? With an uneasy feeling in the pit of his stomach, he crossed his arms, held his breath and stood very still, praying that the strangers would pass them by.

Chapter Eleven:
A Meaty Meeting

Of course, as everyone knows, Gretel passed by nothing, particularly if it was edible. She sighted the open bags of potato chips on the ground and began running toward the brook. You see, she had been walking all day and she was quite hungry.

"Barbeque!" she cried as she sprinted past the three pigs. "Oil and vinegar! Cheddar and onion! Salt and pepper!"

Vowing never to lose his little sister again, Hansel ran after Gretel in a panic. He pushed through the trees. He jumped over a few rocks. He moved up and down, and up and down until BAM! He crashed right into the three plump pigs.

Of course, the crash didn't even move the three plump pigs, being that they were so incredibly heavy. In fact, the first plump pig's cigar never even dropped from his mouth.

Hansel stood and dusted himself off. "Oh my," he said, "I am very sorry. You see, I was trying to catch up to my sister."

The three pigs stood there, frozen, staring at Hansel.

Hansel apologized again. "Did you hear me?" he asked. "I am very sorry."

The second pig pushed the third pig forward. "Say something," he whispered.

Being the bravest, most intelligent pig in the group, the third pig decided that he should try to make peace. "Third pig," he said as he held out his hoof for a shake. "And these are my brothers, second pig and first pig." The second and first pig continued pushing each other forward. Finally the third pig gave up on the introductions.

"So, we were wondering," asked Hansel, "if we could stay at your home for the night." The sun was setting in the west and Hansel and Gretel were too frightened to sleep in the woods alone. They feared that the witch might find them, snatch them up, and eat them for supper. You see, they had no idea that she was now trapped in the stomach of a gigantic bear.

The third pig sighed. "We have no home," he said. "All we have is the bubbling brook." Then he went on to tell Hansel the story of his life. He called it "The Three Plump Pigs and the Big Bad Wolf."

Chapter Twelve:
The Three Plump Pigs
and the Big Bad Wolf

"You see," said the third pig, "there we was, sittin' by the brook, mindin' our own business when my brother, second pig—"

"Yeah, that's me, second pig," interrupted his brother.

The third pig rolled his eyes and continued, "As I was saying," he said, "my brother, second pig, said, 'Let's build a house.' I wanted to build a brick house. But my brother here, you see, he's lazy and hungry all the time. So he said, 'I want to make my house of potato chips and peanut butter.' Can you believe that, *potato chips and peanut butter*? Of course, my other brother, first pig, he agreed with me and said we should make a brick house. So since brick is solid and *not food* like potato chips and peanut butter, we built a brick house. Then, right after we made it, the big bad wolf came along and blew it down with one breath. And that was it. Our house was gone. He even took the bricks with him and built his own house right down that path." He motioned toward a dark, dreary path just south of the bubbling brook.

"And," cried the first pig, "he said he's gonna turn us into fried ham if we ever mess with him again."

After hearing the word "ham," Gretel became interested in the conversation. She tossed the bag of chips and ran over to join the pigs.

"Fried ham?" she asked.

The pigs nodded. "Fried ham!"

Hansel thought about what he had learned on his adventure. He knew what the tortoise would say. He knew what the hare would say.

"Pigs," he said courageously, "you mustn't give up. You must persevere."

"Persasmear?" said the first pig, very confused.

"Persevere!" shouted the third pig. "Never give up!" He turned his head toward Hansel. "So then," he said, "how are *we* gonna get our house back?"

"That's simple," replied Hansel. "It's all a matter of getting in shape!"

And with that, Hansel grabbed a small, pointed stone from the edge of the brook. He spotted an old oak tree a few inches from where the pigs were standing. This particular tree was full of many special carvings, but just left of the heart that read, "Cinderella loves the Prince," he found the perfect spot to carve out his plan.

Chapter Thirteen:
The Right Food
(And That Exercise Stuff)

Hansel carefully carved two circles into the tree.

"You see," he explained, "these circles are for the food groups. This circle is for the grains you eat. Grains like whole wheat bread, whole wheat pasta or oatmeal. These foods give you energy. This next circle is for the meats you eat. Meat like chicken and fish and hamburgers—"

"Mmmm," muttered Gretel, "hamburgers."

Hansel continued. "Meat," he said, "gives you muscles." Then he carved two more circles into the tree. "These circles," he said, "are for fruits and vegetables. You need lots of fruits and vegetables to fight diseases and stay healthy. And then," he continued, as he etched two more circles into the tree, "you need milk  to make your bones strong! If you don't eat from these food groups each day, you will never be strong enough to get your house back. And for Pete's sake," he said as he grabbed the cigar from the first pig's mouth, "you can't keep smoking!"

He tossed the cigar into the brook and turned back toward the group. He had amazed himself! Never before had he been able to think so quickly!

Gretel, of course, was confused. "But Hansel," she cried

as she held up a bag of barbeque chips. "What about chips and cheese curls and cookies and cakes?"

The three pigs nodded their heads and looked toward Hansel.

"Well," said Hansel as he pointed to the last circle on the tree, "this is the fats and oils group. You can eat food from this group, but not all the time."

Gretel and the pigs thought for a moment. Then they sat down by the brook. "Ohhhh," they murmured all together. "Ahhh." They seemed surprised by what they had heard.

The third pig looked up at Hansel very seriously. "All right then," he said. "We'll eat that...that food group stuff. Heck," he said, "we'll even go for a jog every once in a while."

"Me too!" shrieked Gretel.

And so that was that. All of the pigs agreed. If they were going to get back their house, they needed to get in shape.

Chapter Fourteen:
And They Lived Happily Ever After

From that day on, the pigs ate right. They jogged (if you can imagine three plump pigs jogging) and they stopped smoking cigars, which in fact was not at all easy for the first plump pig. Then finally, after a month or so, they no longer were three plump pigs; they had become three strong pigs.

And so they decided that it was finally time to get back their house. They marched down the trail chanting:

"The big bad wolf, he done us wrong,
But now we pigs are big and strong,
We're gonna get that mean old rat,
And send him runnin' like a 'fraidy cat!
Sound off, 1-2
Sound off, 3-4
Sound off, 1-2
3-4!"

49

When they arrived at the wolf's house, Hansel shouted, "Come on out. We would like to talk to you!"

The wolf cried out from inside the house, "Can't you piggies see I am eating a pizza! Now run along!" He stuck his head out of the window. A trail of cheese hung from his lips.

Hansel tried one more time. "We just want to talk to you!" he shouted.

The wolf popped his head back out of the window. "If you piggies don't go," he threatened, "I will be having sausage on my pizza!" Then he shut the window abruptly and continued stuffing his face.

Hansel turned to the group. "Are you ready?" he asked.

The pigs nodded their heads. They felt brave and strong and healthy.

"Ready! Set! Go!" they shouted.

And all together, the five friends blew as hard as they could on the tiny brick house.

They blew!

And they blew!

And they blew!

And then BAM!

The bricks from the house shot out in every direction! The final blast was so strong that the wolf actually shot out of the back of the house and landed in a tree. He may have been able to climb out, but he refused to let go of his extra cheese pizza. And now, just like a poor little insect caught in a spider's web, the big bad wolf was tangled in a mess of mozzarella high up in the forest trees.

Hansel, Gretel and the three pigs rejoiced, for now they had enough bricks to rebuild their home. Hansel helped rebuild the kitchen, Gretel the living room, and the three strong pigs, well, they built five bedrooms: one for each pig, one for Hansel, and one for Gretel.

From that day on, the three strong pigs, Hansel and Gretel lived happily ever after in the wilderness. They ate right, they exercised and every once in a while they split a pack of fried chicken nuggets. And believe me, they lived a very, very long, healthy life.

Food and Fitness Facts for Fairy Tale Lovers

DID YOU KNOW?

Another word for "fats" is "lipids."

Why does "fat" matter?

There are two kinds of fats. "Good" fats help your vision and your heart. But "bad" fats can hurt your heart!

What is a "good" fat?

"Good" fats are found in natural foods like fish, chicken, lean meats, vegetables, nuts and milk.

What is a "bad" fat?

"Bad" fats are found in deep-fried foods, like chicken nuggets, fries, fried cheese sticks and chips. Foods with "bad" fat feel greasy. They may look shiny.

How much fat should I eat?

Don't freak out! You don't have to count fat grams. Just eat right. Eat a variety of foods and beware of greasy snacks or meals.

HOLD THE MAYO!

Mayonnaise is a "bad" fat. There are 11 grams of fat in each tablespoon of mayonnaise. That's a lot! Try mustard, ketchup or salsa instead!

How much fat is in my fries?

Fries are potatoes, but they also contain "bad" fat because they are cooked in fatty oils. This "bad" fat is not good for your heart.

MAKING A BETTER CHOICE

Ask for a baked potato instead of fries! But watch those toppings. Cheese toppings are often loaded with fat. A plain potato with sour cream and chives is a lot healthier than greasy fries!

INSTEAD OF FRIES, CHOOSE CARROT STICKS

Carrots make you strong and keep you healthy! Dip them in cottage cheese for a healthy snack.

How much water do I need?

You should drink about 6-8 glasses of water each day.

How much fat is in my fried chicken?

Remember, just like your fries, fried chicken is cooked in fatty oils. This oil is not heart-healthy or friendly to your body.

MAKING A BETTER CHOICE

Instead of fried chicken, choose grilled, baked or broiled chicken. Here are some better choices:

A broiled chicken sandwich

A broiled chicken salad

A grilled chicken sandwich

WHAT HAPPENED TO THE BIRD

We all know that the bird was eating fried chicken nuggets. These have saturated fat in them. This kind of "bad" fat does not dissolve. It can clog up your arteries and cause problems with your heart. That is why the bird grew weaker and heavier!

How much fat is in my donuts?

Just like French fries, donuts are actually fried in oil. This means that the donuts that you eat for breakfast are not always a healthful choice. Watch out for those donuts that are frosted or sugar-glazed. They are not only high in fat but full of sugar!

Kathryn A. Brave, M.A. and Paul J. Lavin, Ph.D.

MAKING A BETTER CHOICE

Instead of donuts, try low-fat muffins.

How much fat is in my breakfast sandwich?

Some breakfast sandwiches are very healthy. But watch out for those sandwiches that are high in fat. Oftentimes, the biscuits used for breakfast sandwiches are cooked in grease or oil.

MAKING A BETTER BREAKFAST CHOICE

Because biscuits are high in fat, instead try breakfast sandwiches made with English muffins. You could also try plain pancakes, which contain less fat per order!

Believe it or not!

Cereal can be a very healthy breakfast choice. It also fills you with lots of energy!

What about a bagel?

A bagel can be a high-energy, low-fat breakfast choice. A cinnamon raisin bagel is a tasty choice.

INSTEAD OF ICE CREAM, TRY FROZEN YOGURT

A yogurt cone is a healthy dessert choice. Top it with your favorite cereal for a tasty treat!

DON'T FORGET!

Almost everyone needs to enjoy a "fatty" treat once in awhile. Just be sure that when you eat these foods, you eat them in moderation. Better yet, share them with a friend!

DID YOU KNOW?

Vegetables and fruits give you the vitamins that you need to fight diseases and keep you healthy. Eat them in their natural state. Try to avoid fried vegetables.

DID YOU KNOW?

Meat, chicken and fish give you protein. This protein helps you to build your muscles.

DID YOU KNOW?

Milk is a very important part of your diet. Milk provides you with calcium. Calcium keeps your bones strong and healthy.

How much fat is in my potato chips?

Potato chips are crunchy, salty and sometimes spicy. But what you need to remember is that regular potato chips are actually fried in fatty oils. So one serving of about 20 chips is not always healthy.

What about flavored chips?

Flavored chips also contain a high amount of fat. These chips are not only fried in fatty oils, but are often coated with spices that are high in salt content or fat content.

What about corn chips?

Sure, corn chips sound healthy. They are made of corn, right?

Actually, corn chips have more fat in them than potato chips. They are also cooked in fatty oils and should only be eaten in small portions.

But I love chips!

Just make sure that you watch how many chips you eat. Sometimes it is easy to eat more than one serving and not even know it! If you decide to eat fried chips, make sure that you eat one handful, rather than one whole bag!

MAKING A BETTER CHOICE

Try baked potato chips instead of fried chips.

What else can I eat from my school vending machine?

Plain pretzels are always a healthier choice than many other snack chips.

Some trail mixes contain "good" fats from nuts, raisins, and sunflower seeds. Just look out for those mixes that are filled with sweets!

MAKING A BETTER CHOICE

Add ketchup or salsa to your burger for a little zip! Also, mustard and relish are low-fat toppings.

How healthy is my hamburger?

Remember that meat gives you protein. A plain hamburger (with lettuce and tomato) is a much healthier choice than a fried chicken sandwich. But watch the toppings—extra cheese and mayonnaise can pack on the fat!

A HEALTHY SNACK (INSTEAD OF CHIPS)

Spread a rice cake with a tablespoon of peanut butter or low-fat cream cheese. Decorate the cake with carrot pieces, raisins, celery stalks and any other fun, healthy garnishes you would like!

What about pizza?

Pizza can be a very healthy choice. But you need to be sure that the pizza is not saturated in grease and oils. A good test is to blot your pizza with a napkin. See if there is a lot of grease on the pizza. If there is, the pizza may contain a lot of fat!

WATCH THOSE TOPPINGS!

Toppings can add flavor, but some toppings also contain a lot of fat. Try to substitute vegetables for sausage or pepperoni. If you love meat topping, try ham or chicken instead.

AND MOST IMPORTANTLY

Be sure to talk to your doctor and your parents before starting any diet or exercise program. You want to make sure that you are doing everything the healthy way!

Printed in the United States
49758LVS00003B/304-351